HALLOWEEN STEW

To Levi,
Zibble-dee-do
Just for
you —
Enjoy your
book and
share it
too!

Jane
Meyers

Written by Jane Slater Meyers
Illustrated by Cecilia Blomberg

eFrog Press

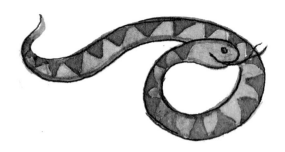

Published by eFrog Press
www.efrogpress.com

ISBN: 978-0-9894356-6-6 (paperback edition)
Library of Congress Control Number: 2015939322

First edition

A tip of the hat to Art, David, Juleen, Jonas, and Kelly for your ideas, words, and constant encouragement. To all our children and grandchildren who bring warmth, surprise, laughter, and a lovely sense of abandon.

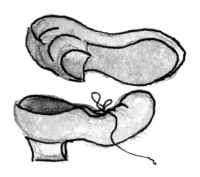

'Round here they call me Mean-Witch-Me.
This stew's all mine so I must flee!
I fly to hunt a hidden spot,
Where I can set my cooking pot.

Each Halloween I cook my stew.
It's all for me and none for you!
With wiggly worms and hopping fleas,
Can't wait to slurp and chomp all these.

Add roots and bones then stir and toil—
See bugs and slugs begin to boil.
My magic bubbles swirl and soar,
Zibble-dibble, zizzy-zor.

Halloween Stew

47 slugs
15 spiders
3 lb. Licorice roots
2 lb. carrots
1 lb bark from dogwood
30 wiggly worms
6 frog legs
1lb dandelion seeds
10 magic bubble seeds
1 lb celery
1 lb potatoes
½ lb mushrooms
3 bay leaves
8 cups dew
¼ lb moss
20 fish heads
red onions
bones

9 chicken fingers
4 lizard tails
7 wings of mosquitos
13 hot peppers
8 fleas
2 heads of garlic
6 apple cores
23 beetle chips

Boil, then simmer gently
until done
Sprinkle with dried ants,
parsley and chopped
horse chestnuts
Enjoy!

With napkin tucked, I eat real fast.
Oh yummy-yum, my stew at last!
As I stuff a bunch of spiders in,
Gobs of sauce drip down my chin.

Ghosts glide this way with flying cats,
Hungry ravens, and swarming bats.
They hover close, they see my stew—
So what's a witch like me to do?

What's that I see? It's not okay!
My bright white bubbles show the way.
Too late to finish up my meal,
With creatures here to snatch and steal.

"Get out! Go away, snoopy crowd.
Howling, cawing, cackling loud."
So what's a witch like me to do?
I'll sneak and fly away from you!

I grab my broom and zoom off fast.
I take my stew, I'll eat at last.
My stew is heavy, full, and hot.
Oh no! I might just drop this pot!

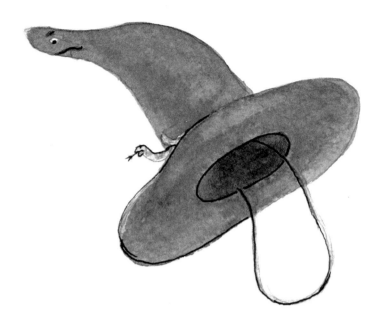

What now? My broom—a snap, a crack!
Down, down by branches, then I *smack*!
I know they watch the crash and see
What happened now to Mean-Witch-Me.

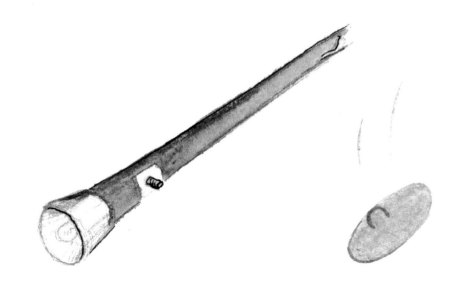

I squat right here with smashed-up toe,
No broom, no stew, nowhere to go.
"Zibble-dee-dibble, zizzy-zor—
My magic words won't work anymore!"

Bats, spiders, turkeys, ghosts, and crows
All creepy-crawl toward my sore nose.
They scream, "Ka-plink, boom-biz-a-boo—
A mean and crabby witch—that's you!"

Now circling close   around poor me,
They dance and spin,   they're on some spree!
"You crush my toe and   snag my sleeve,
Please stop your twirling.   Please just leave!"

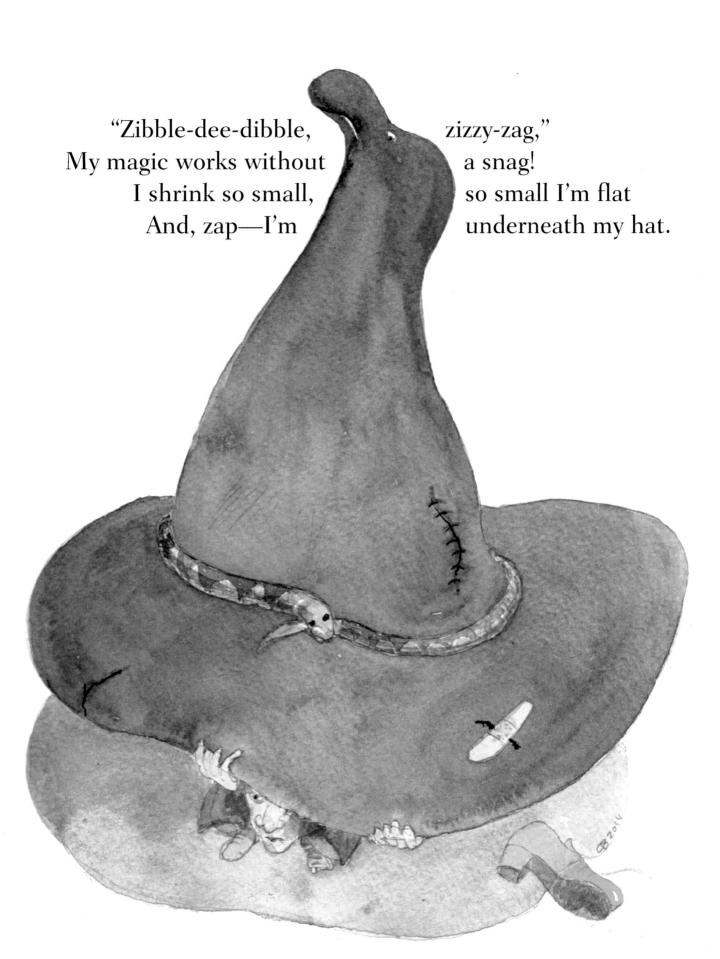

"Zibble-dee-dibble, zizzy-zag,"
My magic works without a snag!
I shrink so small, so small I'm flat
And, zap—I'm underneath my hat.

"Come out and sit under this tree,
We'll share a plan to set you free!
After flying here for yummy stew,
We licked up chunks of soupy-goo!"

"But with no broom,
no way to fly,
You look so much
like you might cry.
It's you who light
our sky with bubbles,
So we will cure
your awful troubles."

"Bippa bappa, zap-zap ka-boom,
Our spell just fixed your broken broom!
With footrest, lights, and speed to spare
Your broom will fly you everywhere."

LED Lights →

switch

Hook for pot

Titanium

foot pedals

Metal rudder twists for steering

Landing sensors

"For me who sneers
and shrieks at you?"
Now, what's a witch
like me to do?
A broom like that—
so strong, so fast,
I think I made
some friends at last!

"Zibbly-zoo! What a switcheroo!
How about flying—me with you?
With my new broom, as you can see,
I am no longer Mean-Witch-Me!"

"One year from now I'll cook more stew
To fill a bowl for each of you.
Our bubbly sky will shine so bright,
When we feast on Halloween Night!"

Halloween Stew Recipe

Directions:

Pour broth, apple juice, and water into a six-quart pot. Prepare ingredients and add all to the pot of liquid. Place the pot on stove and bring to a boil, then simmer for 20 to 25 minutes.

Check rice and root vegetables to make sure they're cooked. Stew will be like soup. Serve in bowls. Enjoy!

Ingredients:

Broth:

4 cups chicken or vegetable broth

2 cups apple juice

1 cup water

The "Yucky" Stuff:

1/2 cup black rice (Thai Jasmine or Indonesian black rice) for bugs and fleas

5 green onions cut 4" inches long with bulb left on for bones, cut in small pieces

1 bunch dark kale leaves (Dinosaur or Lacinto Kale). Cut stems off of 6-8 thinnest leaves with pointy ends—for lizard tails, tear into pieces

1/2 lb. uncooked boneless chicken breast, cut bite-size for frog legs—slide into pot

One 8 oz. jar roasted red pepper, use 1/2 of a roasted red pepper cut ahead of time into long thin pieces for red wiggly worms

1/2 cup small bow-tie pasta for chicken fingers

From the Forest:

5 sage leaves for gathered leaves

1 medium head red leaf lettuce, slice off top red portion for curly moss. Tear 1/2 of the lettuce into small pieces

1 golden or red beet cut in bite-size chunks for roots (red beet will turn broth red)

1 medium potato—cut in bite-size chunks

4 medium carrots—slice in thin rounds

1/2 medium celery root, peel and cut into small pieces

1 fennel bulb with fronds, slice, then dice 1/2 the bulb for licorice roots

1/2 lb. brown mushrooms—clean and cut in half

1 garlic bulb—dice 3 cloves

The Sweeteners:

2 apples peel and cut in ½ inch chunks

2 apple cores—wrap in a cheesecloth bag and place in pot

For more information go to: MyHalloweenStew.com

Jane Slater Meyers enjoyed a varied career in education as an elementary teacher, a reading and language arts coordinator, and an instructional leader in San Diego, California. She originally wrote Halloween Stew for her grandchildren, but friends who read the story said it deserved a bigger audience. Jane's thrilled that Cecilia happily agreed to illustrate Halloween Stew.

Cecilia Blomberg always drew and painted when she was growing up in Sweden. She received formal training as an artist there and has lived in the Pacific Northwest for many years. She works as an artist, mainly designing and weaving tapestries, and squeezes in illustrations when she can.

For story activities and tips for preparing Halloween Stew go to: MyHalloweenStew.com

Made in the USA
San Bernardino, CA
22 September 2015